DATE DUE

SEP 01 2050			
GAYLORD			PRINTED IN U.S.A.

798728   06209B

Look!

Jeff Mack

Philomel Books
An Imprint of Penguin Group (USA)

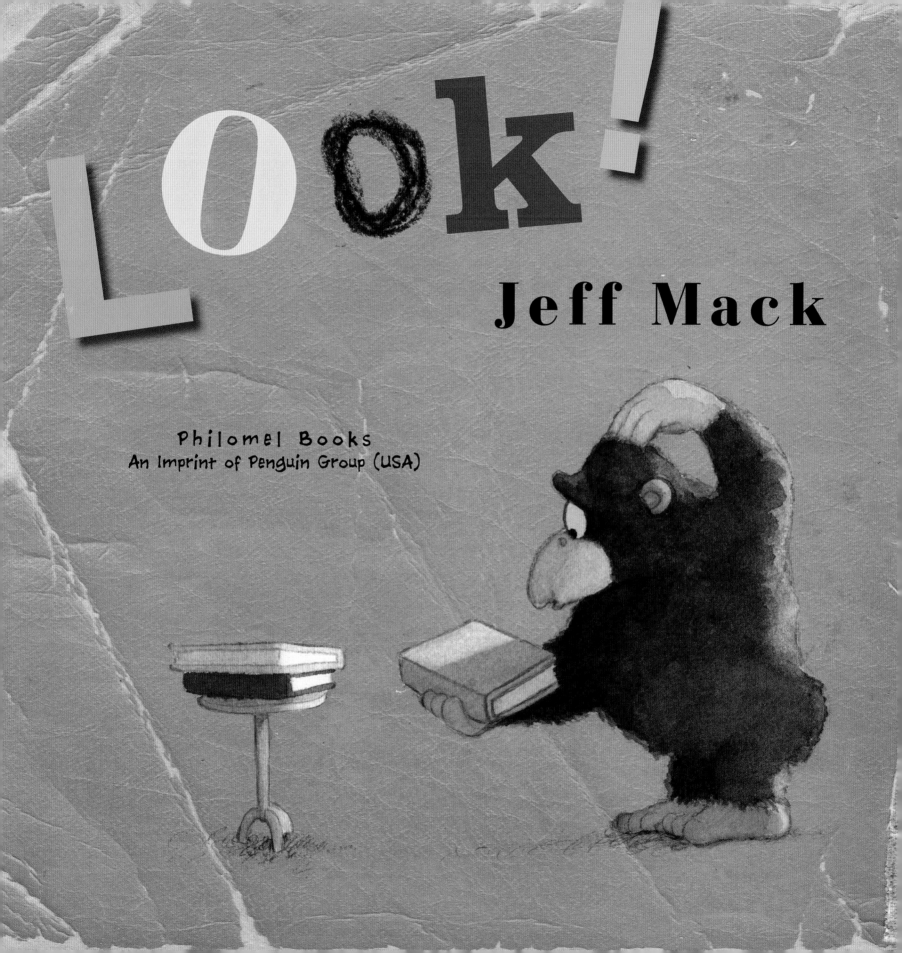

Thank you to my good friends

David Milgrim, Aaron Becker,

and

David Hyde Costello.

PHILOMEL BOOKS
Published by the Penguin Group | Penguin Group (USA) LLC
375 Hudson Street, New York, NY 10014

USA | Canada | UK | Ireland | Australia | New Zealand | India | South Africa | China
penguin.com | A Penguin Random House Company

Copyright © 2015 by Jeff Mack.
Penguin supports copyright. Copyright fuels creativity, encourages diverse voices, promotes free
speech, and creates a vibrant culture. Thank you for buying an authorized edition of this book and
for complying with copyright laws by not reproducing, scanning, or distributing any part of it
in any form without permission. You are supporting writers and allowing Penguin to continue to
publish books for every reader.

Library of Congress Cataloging-in-Publication Data
Mack, Jeff.
Look! / Jeff Mack.   pages cm
Summary: Using only two words—"look" and "out"—relates a story about an attention-loving
gorilla, a television-loving boy, and a friendship that develops over books.
[1. Gorilla—Fiction. 2. Books and reading—Fiction. 3. Friendship—Fiction. 4. Humorous stories.]
I. Title.   PZ7.M18973Lo 2015   [E]—dc23   2014020636
Manufactured in China by South China Printing Co. Ltd.
ISBN 978-0-399-16205-3   10 9 8 7 6 5 4 3 2 1

Edited by Michael Green. | Design by Semadar Megged and Jeff Mack.
The art was created using mixed media, including pencil, watercolor, collage, and digital manipulations.

Look out.

out.

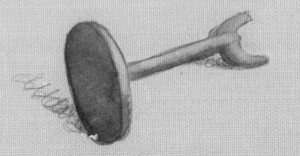

Look.

out.